anything

I0646782

Published in 2016 by **Windmill Books**,
an Imprint of Rosen Publishing
29 East 21st Street, New York, NY 10010

Copyright © 2016 Blake Publishing

Photography: Glenn Brown: p. 15; Dreamstime; Patrick
Honan: IBC (exoskeleton), pp. 6, 14; Steve Parish/
Nature-Connect: front cover, pp. 9, 19–20, 24;
Narinda Sandry: IBC (nymph), pp. 2–3, 7–8, 10, 12.
Photo research: Emma Harm
Cover and text design: Leanne Nobilio
Color management: Greg Harm
Editor: Vanessa Barker

Library of Congress Cataloging-in-Publication Data

Johnson, Rebecca.
Dylan's dragonfly dance / by Rebecca Johnson.
p. cm. — (Bug Adventures)
Includes index.
ISBN 978-1-4777-5615-7 (pbk.)
ISBN 978-1-4777-5614-0 (6 pack)
ISBN 978-1-4777-5538-9 (library binding)
1. Dragonflies — Juvenile literature.
I. Johnson, Rebecca, 1966-. II. Title.
QL520.J683 2016
595.7—d23

Manufactured in the United States of America
CPSIA Compliance Information: Batch WS15WM: For Further Information
contact Rosen Publishing, New York, New York at 1-800-237-9932

Bug Adventures

CONTENTS

Who would have
thought something
ugly like me,
could one day
turn into a nice
thing to see?

Who would have known
that my home in this pond,
was just at the start
of my life far beyond?

My mom laid an egg
on the side of a reed,
with water all around
and the food that I need.

And then, when I hatched,
I looked around to see,

the water was filled with nymphs just like me.

to stay out of sight
of birds up above.

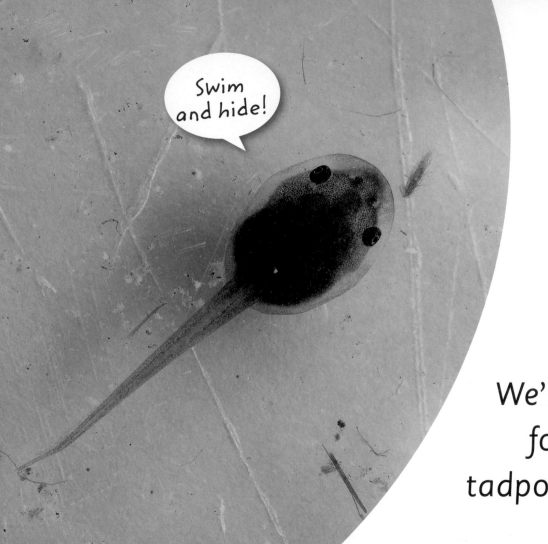

We're hunting
for fish and
tadpoles to eat.

10

For us, lots of small creatures are a treat.

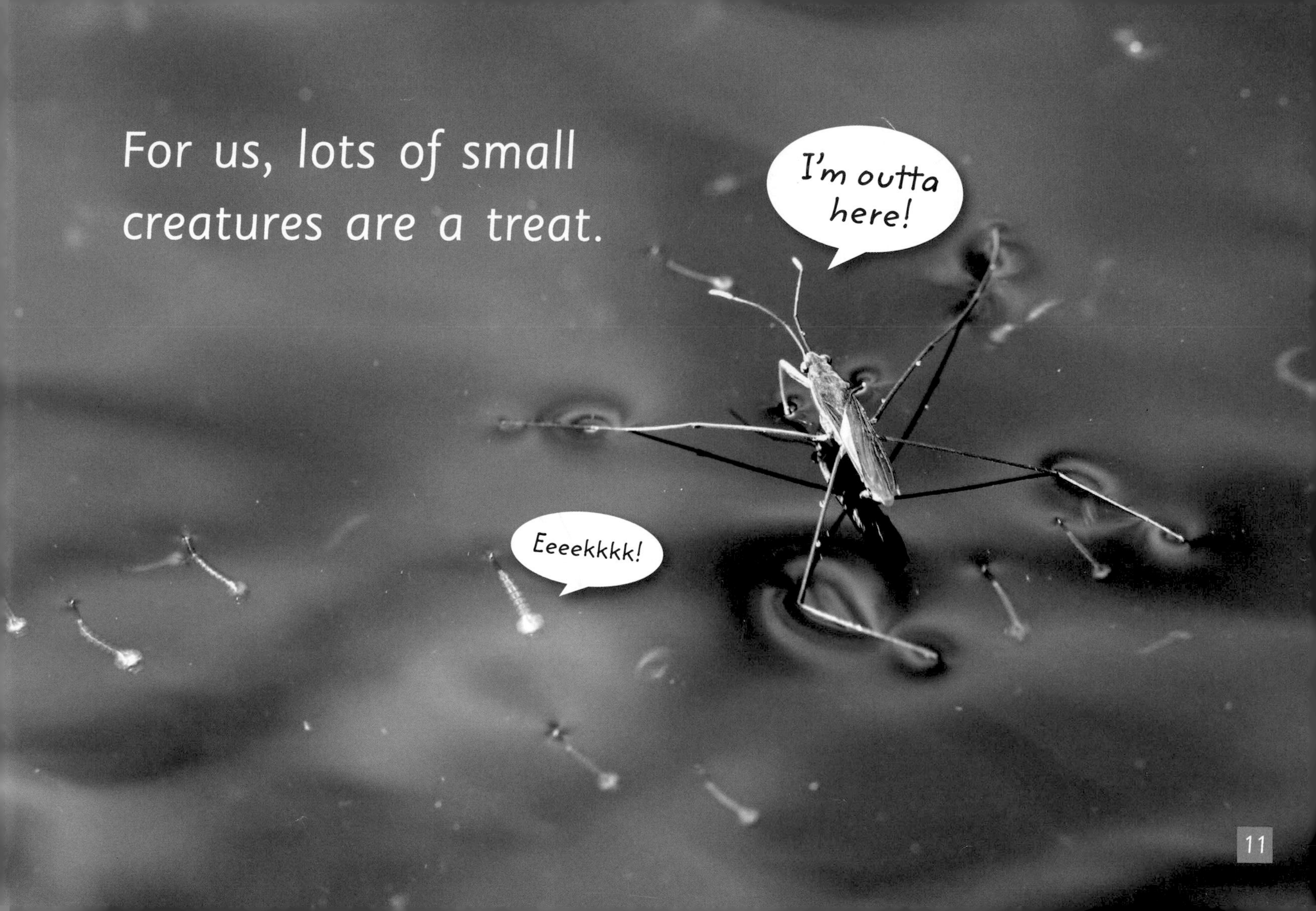

Molting twelve
times and leaving behind,
exoskeletons that you might find.

Years later on,
my molting
is done,

and my last stage
has finally begun.

14

My colors come
out as I climb
from below.

15

I spread my wings and off I go.

Forwards and back, we fly side to side.

Most cannot catch us, there's no need to hide.

19

We catch flies
and mosquitoes
while still in the air,

we hover and dive,
with grace and with flair.

21

We find our mates
and start again,

22

this cycle of life
that has no end.

After just a few months,
our time is done.
A dragonfly's life
is an interesting one!

24

Dragonfly

① Adult — Dragonfly

④ Molting from exoskeleton

Life Cycle

② Eggs

③ Nymph